WILL and STACIE #4:

THE LOST COAL MINE

by Oak Blackheart

Edited by Jo Smith

DEDICATION

This story is dedicated to the friends, classmates and teachers at Wilburton Schools, who had a great influence and shared molding me in the early years. You may or may not see yourself in my stories, but there is a piece of many of you here and there. Thank you my friends.

ACKNOWLEDGEMENT

Nancy Parker, who is my life partner, my inspiration and joy, is my advisor in much of the content in the stories and my life.

There is a special thank you to Jo Ann Graham Smith, friend and classmate, for all her help in editing my stories. Any mistakes you might find are my inadequacy in correcting what had been suggested.

CONTENT

PROLOGUE

Mrs. Robinson asked. "Where are you going?"

We're headed down to the bridge. We want to cut red willow branches to make baskets," Stacie told her mother.

"What, Will Ballad, you want Stacie to show you how to make baskets?"

"Knowledge is a wonderful thing, Mrs. Robinson. The more I know the stronger it makes me. Who knows when I might need the skill?"

The hot, dog days of August were here. It had been over 100°F for the last week. Trees along the road were tinted red from the iron rich Oklahoma earth. The air was dry, and the scent of pine filled your nose. Heat waves rose in the distance, and it was still early.

Stacie and Will let their bikes roll down the big hill. Stacie laughed as they crossed the bridge, "Do you remember saving me after I was swept off the bridge, Will?"

Two years ago Stacie was almost lost in a flood, when they tried to cross a low water bridge on their way home. The creek was in flood stage, and Stacie washed off the bridge. Stacie grabbed a willow tree that had been close to the edge of the lazy creek the day before. Today the tree was in the middle of the fast moving river. She clung to the tree as Will ran back and plunged into the dark churning water, grabbing hold of a willow, climbing hand over hand to reach Stacie, and bending one tree top to the next. Stacie grabbed hold of Will's leg and pulled herself up until she could reach his hand. He pulled on Stacie's arm and the swift turbulent current pulled on both of them. Finally Stacie got to the tree top that Will held. They moved together from willow to willow until they reached the safety of the bank. Will laughed with her saying, "We were really lucky that day."

Will and Stacie laid their bikes on the bank and waded into the water. Stacie demonstrated how to cut the willow branches and strip the leaves. After they cut 30 branches each, they bundled them into one bunch. Pank, Will's brother, was driving now, so he would be happy to drive down to pick up the willow branches.

Stacie looked at the pavilion, in the Colony's little picnic area, which was built by the WPA (Works Progress Administration and it was renamed Work Projects

Administration in 1939.) during the depression. It was made from native stone and large pine timbers. Picnic tables were inside. "It looks like a person is lying on the table, Will," Stacie said, "Let's go look."

It was a short bike ride to the pavilion. A woman lay on the table. There was some blood on the left side of her face. There was more blood on the table and the floor of the pavilion.

Will felt for a pulse with his hand across her neck. "She has a pulse," Will said.

Stacie shook her. "Hey! Are you all right? She's breathing." Still there was no response. Stacie said "Don't put your hand over her Adam's apple. If she comes to she may think you're strangling her. Touch her on the closest side to find her pulse."

"That's one of the Sawyer twins, but is it Sadie or Sydney?" Will asked.

Stacie said, "I don't know. Go get help. I'll stay here."

Chapter 1

THE MYSTERY

Will could see Mrs. Rita Miller was in her yard. It was a short ride across the bridge and a right turn to her driveway. He rode right up to her.

"Hi Will. How are you? Where is Stacie?"

"Mrs. Miller, One of the Sawyer twins is unconscious at the pavilion. Can you call an ambulance and Deputy Sheriff Hawthorne? I'm heading back to help Stacie." Marc Hawthorne was a friend of Will and Stacie's, and he lived in the colony. Marc had married Miss Daisy Flowers, their favorite teacher last year, and Marc helped capture Hank Grabber, who a newspaper reporter dubbed the Bicycle Bandit. He was a purse snatcher on a bicycle.

Sheriff Latimer was impressed with Marc's performance and made Marc a deputy sheriff.

Mrs. Miller said, "I'll make the calls," she turned and walked briskly toward the house.

Stacie repositioned the Sawyer twin in a more comfortable position, and placed a wet bandana across her forehead. Mrs. Miller and Marc arrived a few minutes before the ambulance rolled up to the pavilion.

Stacie and Will told Marc how they discovered the woman and what they did. Marc went to retrieve Stacie's bandana. Marc and the ambulance driver, Roger Adams, loaded the unconscious girl into the ambulance.

Marc had secured the area, and he had Will and Stacie write their statements, explaining how and when they discovered the Sawyer twin. Sheriff Latimer drove up with his siren screaming and lights flashing.

Sheriff Latimer laughed and frowned before he smiled when he saw the detective duo. "What did you two stumble into this time?"

Will quickly told the story again, and Marc told the Sheriff that he had their statements. Sheriff Latimer said, "If I need more information, you will have to come to my office." He cut them loose.

Will and Stacie started for the main road. "Will, let's go to the Sawyer's place and see if the other twin is there." They lived in a small rent house south of the colony on Oklahoma State Highway 2 about a mile away. Once they were on pavement, the pair pedaled hard. Five minutes later Will and Stacie were at the driveway. The house was hidden in a thick post oak forest. Half way up the rough gravel driveway, they could see two cars were parked in front of the house. Dropping the bikes, they entered the yard and knocked on the door.

The door opened and a 23 year old blonde stood before them. Will smiled and said, "Hi Sydney."

"I'm Sadie," she said. "What are you two up to this morning?"

Stacie had been thinking of what to ask whoever opened the door. She didn't want to seem nosy. They had to tell Sadie the news, if she didn't know about Sydney, or at least they didn't think she knew that Sydney had been banged on the head and found unconscious on a picnic table. Finally Stacie spoke, "We discovered Sydney unconscious on a picnic table in the pavilion at the colony entrance."

Sadie's smile left her face, and she turned pale. "I have been worried about her. She wasn't home when I woke up. I went to bed early last night. She must have gone for a walk. She does that, sometimes, walks late at night when she wants to think.

"We saw her on the table and went to investigate. Sheriff Latimer and Deputy Sheriff Hawthorne are at the pavilion now," Stacie said.

"Where is Sydney now?" Sadie asked.

Will said, "The ambulance is taking her to the McAlester Hospital."

"I have to go to her. I have to call our folks." Sadie was frantic as she spoke.

Stacie said, "Please keep us in the loop on her condition. If there is anything we can do to help, just let us know. I know she will be all right."

As Will and Stacie left, the Sheriff and Marc turned up the driveway. Sheriff Latimer stopped, "What are you doing here?"

Will said, "We told Sadie that Sydney was taken to the Hospital."

"This is an active investigation. Both of you need to leave this to the professionals. Go home and don't get run over on the highway."

Will said,"Okay." The two amateur detectives were off. They could see the pavilion area had been secured with tape as they entered the Colony.

Jeremy Sean Campbell said, "Hey Will, what happened here?" He was sitting on his sister's paint (pony) and studying the pavilion. Jeremy Sean Campbell was a wild hooligan who lived by the Damon Schoolhouse. He had graduated from high school this spring. Jeremy and Will hunted raccoons in the winter.

Stacie told Jeremy how Sydney was found unconscious on the table.

Jeremy Sean said, "Who did it?"

"We don't know. Sadie didn't even know her sister was gone. Her car was parked at the house. She either walked or someone picked her up," Will stated.

Jeremy Sean looked puzzled, "Do they have any clues? Who are the suspects?"

"We know nothing. Sheriff Latimer and Marc are investigating. They're not talking," Stacie said.

"I better get moving," Jeremy Sean said, and wheeled the pony and trotting off.

"We can't look around; the area is secured. Let's go back and tell the folks," Stacie said. The two rode to Will's house to share their story, but word had spread through the colony via the party line.

"Pank would you drive down to the bridge and pick up our red willow branches? We'll go with you," Will said."Let's go. We can take the truck. Let me get the keys," Pank replied.

Pank was still in the house when Mrs. Black came up the driveway wringing her hands. "Will, can you get my kitten down? She climbed a telephone pole and is afraid to come down. I know a hawk will swoop down and pluck her right off the top of the pole." Will said, "Sure, Mrs. Black. Let me changed shoes. I can climb poles like islanders climb coconut palm trees." Will went to the garage and came out with two ropes. One was his safety line and the other was tied in a loop. Will, Stacie and Pank walked with Mrs. Black to the road. The cat was in plain sight on top of the telephone pole.

Will put his feet in the small loop. There was enough space between his feet that he could stand with the pole almost in-between his feet. Then the safety line was tied so he could lean back and still touch the pole with his hands. It was simple to climb; lock your feet on the pole, jump the safety line up then jump your feet up. You would repeat the pattern until you reach the top. It was a little trickier coming down. He had to be quick with his feet, or he would slide down until the safety line would catch.

Will would joke saying, "Don't try this at home. It requires a trained professional."

Will made it look simpler than it was. At the top the kitten jumped on Will's shoulder and almost caused him to lose his purchase on the pole. The timid kitten then ran down his right pant leg and down the pole, jumping the last ten feet. Mrs. Black was happy, and she repeated herself more than once. "Boots you're a bad kitty. Boots would still be up there if it wasn't for you, Will. Thank you so much."

Will carefully worked his way down the pole. He said, "It's quicker to climb up a pole than to come down."

Pank started back for the truck. "Wait up, Pank I'll walk with you. I have to change shoes," Will said. Stacie stayed so she could talk to Mrs. Black about her cat. It wasn't long before Pank stopped on the road; Stacie climbed in the front with Will and Pank. They brought the willow branches back, and Stacie curled the willows in a wash tub to soak and soften.

Will and Stacie headed to the Robinson's home on top of the hill. Mrs. Robinson was fixing lunch and asked Will to stay. The conversation at lunch was centered on Sidney Sawyer. After lunch Will and Stacie went back to the bridge. Oklahoma State Bureau of Investigation (OSBI) had a panel truck at the pavilion. Will and Stacie rode to the crime scene tape to watch the men.

"Let's ride along the creek road and see what's at the dam," Stacie said.

The road was dry and sandy. You could see several sets of footprint in the road. At the dam, Stacie spotted a gold watch with a broken band.

"Stacie, look here! It's a clutch," Will exclaimed. He picked it up and opened it to see whose it was. "Stacie this is Sydney's." It had a drivers license, pictures, voter registration card and a twenty dollar bill with the ink smudged and running. "That twenty has to be counterfeit, ink doesn't run on real bills," Will said.

"Leave it there, Will. We need to tell the OSBI men at the pavilion."

Will and Stacie rode back to the pavilion being very careful to stay on the edge of the sandy road and avoid the footprints in the sand.

Stacie was excited to have another mystery to solve. "We have to be behind the scenes on this, Will. Sheriff Latimer has all ready warned us to stay out of this since it is an active case."

The crime scene guys were as excited as Will and Stacie when they heard about the watch and the clutch. The older man said, "Jim you go with the kids and see what they found. Take the camera and get pictures of the footprints."

"Jim Jacobs is my name. What are your names?"

"I'm Will Ballad, and this is Stacie Robinson." Everyone said, "I'm glad to meet you," almost at the same time.

The three walked down the road toward the dam. Jim was careful to take pictures of the tracks. He placed a ruler by the footprints. When Mr. Jacobs saw the corner of the twenty dollar bill in Sydney's clutch he confirmed Will and Stacie's suspicions. Jacobs said, "That's a counterfeit twenty."

Jim Jacobs pulled out a roll of line and tied one end to a tree close to the creek bank. He handed the roll to Will and directed him to tie the line to a tree on the far side of the road. It was plain to Will and Stacie that Officer Jacobs didn't want to get his feet wet. The creek washed around the westside of the dam. "Tie the line to that big tree, and then take the line across the dam. Will, tie the line to the redbud tree. Bring it back and throw the line to me," Jacobs said. When they were finished, the line completed a four sided polygon.

Jacobs said, "Thank you for the help. You found some key evidence. Let's go back to the pavilion. John and I will come back and work this area after we finish with the pavilion."

John marked the road as a crime scene to secure the road to the dam.

Will and Stacie already knew someone was passing counterfeit twenty dollar bills. Bad twenties were popping up all over Latimer County and the surrounding area. Bob Trout, a new resident in the colony was also interested in the person who was passing these counterfeit twenties.

Everyone in the Veteran Colony had a military background or their spouse was a veteran. Trout was retired Air Force. He had started out in the Army Air Corp in World War II and flew during the Korean Conflict. Robert Trout seemed like a good guy. He and Pank would talk about flying. Mr. Trout was very interested in Pank's radio controlled airplanes.

Trout's friend, Jake Brown, who lived in Buffalo Valley, was selling a Colt Woodman semi automatic .22 to a stranger, who said his name was George Johnson. The stranger wouldn't give Jake any twenty dollar bills. Jake went with Johnson to a gas station, a grocery store and a feed store to break the twenties before he would pay Jake for the Colt. All three businesses came up with counterfeit twenties.

Brown described George Johnson as tall, maybe six foot three, thin, with black curly hair and a very smooth talker. Stacie worked busing tables at the the Green Frog in Wilburton and sometimes as a waitress. She was keeping an eye out for the stranger who called himself George Johnson.

Isabella Rose Martinez, whose friends call her Buckle, was on Thunder, a horse both black and brown, rode up in the Ballad's driveway to see what was happening. Pank walked out the front door to see why Shag was barking. Pank whistled and said, "Shag come here." Shag came up to the porch immediately. Pank scratched his ears then Shag soon lay on the porch to watch Buckle and Thunder. "What's going on with you, Buckle?" Pank asked.

"We're out and about this afternoon." Isabella was careful not to say or even lead Pank to suspect that she came to see Will. Buckle had good people skills, and would look you in the eye and make you feel that you were the most important person in the world. "What have you been doing?"

"I've been working on some trigonometry problems," Pank said.

"School's out, big guy," Isabella reminded him.

"I know. I'll be enrolled in a trig class when school starts. I want to be ahead of the game."

Isabella dismounted and Pank walked with her and Thunder to a grassy area in the yard. Isabella left the reins over Thunder's neck, attached a lead rope to the bridle, and dropped it. Thunder would stay there and feed on the grass.

Pank told Isabella about Sydney Sawyer. "Get your bike and follow me home and we'll go to the pavilion for a look-see," Isabella said. It was understood that Isabella was going to ride her bike. Pank was excited to ride with Buckle. Half way around the colony they met Will and Stacie.

"Hey, guys! What's up?" Isabella said. "We want to see the pavilion."

Stacie said, "Okay let's get going. We found Sidney's watch and clutch by the dam. The OSBI is searching for

evidence. Sydney had a counterfeit twenty in her clutch."
Stacie was sorry she spoke so quickly; She had wanted
to keep that clue to herself and Will.

Pank and Buckle were pedaling hard to stay ahead.
Anytime you put two bikes together, you have a race.
Soon the group was crossing the bridge. The panel truck
was still there, but the crime scene guys were nowhere in
sight. Stacie said, "They must be at the dam. Let's go in
the back way to see what they are doing." Stacie wants to
be a detective, and she wanted to know how they were
processing the facts they discovered.

The OSBI men, John and Jim, were making plaster casts
of footprints in the mud. Jim Jacobs saw them behind the
dam and called them over. "I need to take pictures of your
shoe soles to be able to rule you out." He looked at Pank
and Isabella asking, "Were you two here recently?" Pank
and Isabella both said, "No." The smaller man took
pictures of Will and Stacie's shoe soles while Jim held a
ruler.

The two OSBI men searched the area and found nothing
more. Jim said, "We're going to leave for now. The area is
still secured. We may be back. If not, I'll call the Sheriff
and he will open the area. Don't enter the crime scene

area. We appreciate your help and cooperation. Keep your eyes open. Thanks again."

The next day Buckle showed up on her bike at the Ballad's house. Stacie and Will were stripping the bark off of the willow branches. Buckle asked if she could help and Pank came out to help, also. The work was quick and before long all the branches were stripped clean. Stacie said, "We can start the baskets after supper tonight. Let's go explore east of Scotty's Cabin."

Pank said, "I'm in."

Will, Stacie, Buckle and Pank rode to Scotty's Cabin. The route was well worn. Will and Stacie had been riding it for three years." The trail starts just over the saddle of that hill. I call it a deer trail,"Will said. It was a single track, only wide enough to ride single file. Stacie led the way. It was fast. There were a few limbs that would slap you in the face. The trail twisted and turned with climbs and downhills. After an hour, Stacie stopped, "Where do you think we are?"

Pank said, "We have been going east and northeast. My guess is that we are on the east side of Yourman Ranch."

Mr. Yourman was a jeweler and watch repairman that worked for the Army Air Force during World War II. He worked on the airplanes' instruments, gauges and clocks. His father was an avid hunter who imported Russian Boars and other exotic animals. Buckle pointed off the trail and said, "Look there is a small pool of water." Will was the first one to the pool. "This is a spring. See the water seeping out of the ground. It's bound to be good water. Look at all the tracks."

Stacie knelt down and tasted the water. "It's good water." They all got a good drink of water.

Pank said, "Look there, it looks like mine tailings. Let's go take a look." A good hundred yards down the gentle slope there was a pile of coal slag.

Leaving the bikes at the spring the small group walked down to the slag pile. Buckle went behind some thick bushes, and after a few minutes we heard her say, "Come see what I have found."

Stacie was the first one there and she said, "It's a coal mine." Will and Stacie always carried signal mirrors. "Will, get your mirror out and hit me with a beam." Will shot a sunbeam and Stacie reflected it in the mine. Pank and Buckle walked in and discovered a small manual printing press. They switched places and Will and Stacie went in the mine.

"How do you think it got here?" Buckle said.

Will said, "They didn't come the way we did."

Pank started looking around. There was a dry creek bed about hundred yards down the hill. Pank walked down to the creek bed then started back up quickly. "Grab your bikes we need to hide. Someone is coming."

The group scrambled for their bikes. They rode back the way they had come until they were well out of sight. Their hearts were pounding with excitement. "Do you think we were seen?" Will questioned.

Pank said, "Probably not. Where's Stacie?"

"Her bike is here," Will said. Stacie had gone back to see who was coming. Will crept down the trail. Stacie was peeking from behind a tree, and motioned for him to stay back. After a minute, which seemed like an hour, Stacie came back to Will and they both ran back to Pank and Buckle.

Pank said, "It was an old red pickup truck. Did you see anyone?"

"I don't think he saw me. He stopped too far back for me to identify him. He has to be the counterfeiter though. He was tall and thin with black hair," Stacie said. The information left everyone excited and apprehensive. Stacie said, "We had better get back and tell the Sheriff what we found."

With the adrenalin flowing, it was a quick trip back.

Pank called the Sheriff and passed on the information. An hour later Marc and Deputy Jerry Jones drove up to the Ballad's house. "We can't find the coal mine on any maps," the deputy said. "You are going to have to show me where the trail starts." They were excited to go. Marc broke their balloon. "Pank is our point of contact. The rest of you can't come. Jerry will bring Pank back," Marc stated. Pank sat in the middle of Jerry Jones' truck. At Scotty's cabin Pank led them up to the saddle and showed Marc the trail. Luckily Marc had a pack with food, water and a radio. Back at the truck Jerry did a radio check while Marc was on the saddle, but below the hill the signal was quickly lost.

Pank said, "The radio is line of sight."

"I'll be able to pick it up on the Yourman Ranch once I get over there." Deputy Jones said.

Marc Hawthorne had an impressive army record. He was part of an elite team of Long Range Reconnaissance Patrol that were part of the 11th Airborne Division which would go behind the borders of the Soviet Block Countries of Czechoslovakia and East Germany. Three years ago there was a rumor that Marc had a whiskey still in the woods. Marc and his dog, Duke, might spend a week hiking in the backwoods and cover as much as thirty miles before coming back.

Just a little over an hour passed when Deputy Jerry Jones dropped Pank at the house.

Buckle asked, "Pank, where's Marc?"

"Marc is walking the trail to the mine. Then he is going to walk out the same way the truck drove to the mine," Pank stated.

Stacie said, "Marc's fast; he can stay with us on our bikes in the woods."

It was the middle of the afternoon when Mrs. Ballad called the children in to drink water and eat a quarter cup of dry, raw oatmeal as a low sugar snack. They then went outside where Stacie started helping the kids weave baskets. "Starting the baskets is the tricky part, then you just follow the pattern," Stacie said. "You can pull up the roots of buck berry bushes when the ground is soft. The roots will go for fifteen or twenty feet. Buck berry roots are good to make larger baskets."

Mrs. Ballad tapped on the window and said, "Stacie you have a phone call."

Stacie came outside. It was hard to read the expression on her face. "I will be working 10-2 tomorrow at the Green Frog. I'll make good tips, but I want to be off until school starts and then work weekends," she said.

Will said, "That's a bummer." Pank's and Buckle's disappointment showed on their faces.

Right then Marc and Jerry drove up to the house. Marc said, "I found the spring and the mine. It was empty. The shaft drops straight down just a little ways back. It will have to be blocked off. Whoever had the press in the mine has packed up everything. It was easy to follow the tracks in the dry creek to a pasture road and then the main ranch road. I asked Jack Nettles if he or his family knew who had been on the road. They hadn't seen anyone on the road, nor did they know that there was an old coal mine bordering near the ranch. It wasn't on the Yourman Ranch property."

Pank said, "It sounds like a lost mine to me."

Chapter 2

Will and Stacie had worked three days a week all summer. They were taking off August, until school started, then they would work Saturdays after school started. Stacie was called in because two of the three waitresses would be off for the noon rush. Will was riding into town with Stacie. He would go by the bike shop to see if Leigh needed any help. If not, maybe he could check with his friends to catch up on what they had been doing.

Stacie brought up some interesting questions. "Why is the counterfeiter hanging out in Latimer County? How did he know about the mine?"

Will said, "He must have grown up in the area. We can talk to Nellie Beltz. She knows all the people that have lived on our side of Blue Mountain." Nellie Beltz lived on the highway two miles north of the colony. "Stacie, we can stop and talk to her on our way home."

Stacie left her bike in back of the restaurant, "Will, meet me here at two," then she went inside to change clothes before she went to work."See you, girl. Have fun." Will answered.

Will went to the bike shop. Leigh Chambers had a sign in the window: Closed. Mr. Chambers was the shop teacher at the high school. He was probably working at school. Leigh would open the shop week days after school by appointment only. On Saturdays Leigh and Will worked 10 a.m. to 2 p.m. at the shop. Will rode to the edge of town remembering the chase with the Bicycle Bandit.

Will thought, oh man, Stacie and I have had some adventures. She is my best friend, and I would do anything for her.

On the way to school Will saw Miss Judy Raindrop out in her yard. Miss Raindrop was the music teacher at school. She was young and attractive. Without a doubt she was the most popular teacher in the whole school. When Judy Raindrop smiled and giggled the whole class would sit up straighter and sing with all their hearts.

"Hi, Miss Raindrop," Will called out, and Miss Raindrop said, "Hi, Will. How are you?" Will stopped and said, "You looked as if you are in deep thought." Will thought this was a little bold to say to a teacher, but since Miss Raindrop seemed like an older version of a close friend, he decided to take a chance, and said, "A penny for your thoughts."

A big bright smile spread across Miss Raindrop's face. A musical giggle erupted from her throat. "Will, I've lost several things in July and August. For the life of me, I have no idea where they are."

Will thinks, Stacie will turn this into a major mystery to solve. A smile creeps out on his face, as he thought of Stacie's excitement at a new mystery. "What kind of things have you lost?"

"My Grandmother's gold coin necklace disappeared first, then, a sterling silver friendship ring disappeared that I had since I was a little girl. Now, a gold charm bracelet is gone. Diana is my best friend. We each bought them just alike when we were in the sixth grade, because we would be friends forever. I continued to buy charms or my family give me charms all the way through high school. There are many fond memories attached to the missing pieces of jewelry."

"Are you sure you didn't misplace them?" "I might have misplaced one item, but I'm a creature of habit. I keep everything in its place, and everything has its place."

"I read a story where a packrat was stealing jewelry. Do you think you may have a rodent robber?"

"That's a possibility; I don't have any mice or rats," Judy Raindrop said.

"That's going to be tough to find. Do you think your house has been broken into?" Will asked.

"No. I always lock the doors and nothing else is missing. If someone would break in, wouldn't they take it all at one time? It would be too risky to come back every week, and take this one time and that the next."

"If it's okay, Stacie and I will come back and investigate later this afternoon."

Miss Raindrop giggled and said, "Sure come on over. I may be out. Catch me if you can."

Will had to laugh. Judy Raindrop is a friend and a teacher at school. Will thought, I would never dare talk to her at school as freely as I do here. It would be Miss Raindrop and business all the way.

Miss Raindrop lived in her Grandmother's house. It was more of a mansion than a house. The house was not in disarray, but with a small imagination—one word "haunted". It was built at the turn of the century. Her house had a huge yard with multiple out buildings, in good condition. There were tin ceilings in every room. Will wondered where were the pieces of jewelry? Lost? Misplaced? Stolen? Will headed to the high school. Mr. Chambers was at the shop, when Will arrived.

"Hi Will. What are you doing in town today?" Mr. Chambers asked.

"Stacie was called in to work, and I rode in with her."

"Have you heard any news on Sydney Sawyer's condition? Is she still in the hospital?" Mr. Chambers asked.

"Mom said that she is still unconscious. The Sheriff thinks it has something to do with the counterfeiters that are passing phony twenties out in the county, Mr. Chambers."

"I hope she will be all right. Can you help me tape this truck? I have to paint it before school starts and get it out of here." Leigh and Will worked through lunch, and they finished just before 2:00.

Stacie was working the counter during lunch hour, when a tall thin man with black curly hair sat down. Stacie's antennas went up immediately. Stacie set a glass of water and menu down. The man said, "Coffee, please." Stacie returned with a cup of coffee and took his order.

Stacie thought about what she would ask this man. Stacie returned with his chicken fried steak and started a conversation. "Are you new in town?"

"I'm here for the day, maybe two days."

"What's your name?"

"John Brown."

Stacie said, "Ask me again and I'll knock you down."

John Brown laughed, "I'm the one who is suppose to say that."

Stacie laughed and gave him her giant smile that lit up his face in a smile, too.

"Your kind of young to be working here."

"I'm filling in as a waitress. I bus tables three days a week. Where are you from?"

"Denver, just traveling through. I heard the Kiowa Indians wintered south of Wilburton. I'm buying arrowheads and guns when I can find them."

"That's interesting work. Do you sell them? Or do you have a collection? And do you have any arrowheads from here?"

"I collect, and I sell, if I can make a profit, and no, but the day's not over yet," John Brown chuckles at his reply.

Jimmy was at the cash register. He looked at Stacie and said in his thick Greek accent, "Mother them, Stacie, mother them."

"I've got to go." Stacie started with refills on the coffee and water. She made her way to Jimmy and whispered, "Watch the guy with the black curly hair that I was talking to. He matches the description of the man who passed counterfeit twenties in Buffalo Valley."

She wrote tickets for the customs who had finished and bused the counter. By the time Stacie was back to John Brown, he was ready for his ticket too. Stacie tore out his ticket, if that was his real name. "Will I see you tomorrow?

"Maybe." Mr. Brown waited until a table of six men got up. Nonchalantly Brown beat them to the register to pay with his long strides. The six men were lined up behind him. Brown handed the ticket and twenty to Jimmy.

Jimmy looked at the bill and said, "This looks like funny money. Where did you get it?"

"I sold a gun to a man in Red Oak. He gave the twenty to me."

"You need to call the Treasury Department, or take it down to the bank," Jimmy said.

Mr. Brown grabbed the bill from Jimmy, threw down $3.00, and walked out without waiting for his change.

A man in line said, "Isn't that the Treasury man in the back booth?"

Mr. Brown acted as if he didn't hear the man speak as he left.

Stacie went to the window and watched Mr. Brown back the blue Chevrolet pickup truck out and drive away. Stacie couldn't read the license plate covered with mud, but what she could see didn't look like a Colorado tag.

"Jimmy, did the guy give you a counterfeit twenty?" Stacie ask.

"He tried, but thanks to you I didn't take it," Jimmy said.

Jimmy finished with the last customers in line. The restaurant was beginning to clear out. The man from the last booth approached Jimmy. He identified himself as a Treasury man showing his badge and I.D.

Jimmy, Stacie and the Treasury man, Jack Pratt, stood at the cash register and talked for a few minutes. Pratt got the description as well as all the other information Stacie had to offer. Jack Pratt went to the phone, called the Oklahoma Highway Patrol, and put out an All Points Bulletin (APB). The Oklahoma Highway Patrol would notify all the law enforcement officials to be on the lookout for a late model blue Chevrolet pickup truck, and John Brown aka (also known as) George Johnson. He is 6 foot 3 inches tall, weighs 190 pounds with black curly hair and blue eyes.

Stacie worked quickly filling the napkin holders and salt, pepper and sugar containers for the evening crowd. Soon, her shift was over. Stacie was satisfied with her performance for the day. She changed clothes and went out the back door for her bike. Will was just riding up to the Green Frog. Stacie quickly told him what took place in the restaurant.

Will told Stacie of the Raindrop mystery. It did not seem to be as important to her at the moment as Will thought it would've been. Stacie was still focused on John Brown and foiling the attempt made to pass a counterfeit twenty.

Headed back home, Stacie said, "Let's stop and talk with Nellie Beltz, and see if she knows anything about the stranger, John Brown, and the coal mine.

Nellie Beltz was a 90 year old German lady who had immigrated to the United States in 1875. This petite lady in a calico dress with white hair up in a bun answered the door, and she was surprised to see Stacie and Will. Stacie said, "Nellie, you know Will Ballad. He lives in the Colony in the old Ford place."

Nellie Beltz said, "Yes, I remember Will. It's nice to see you again. How is your mother, Stacie?"
"She is fine Mrs. Beltz." "You two come into the kitchen. You look tired and thirsty. You need a glass of water." Nellie went to the refrigerator for a pitcher of cold water. "Stacie, the glasses are in the cupboard by the sink. Would you get three glasses, please."

"Are these jelly glasses okay?"

"Yes, they will be fine, Stacie. Please sit down. I've not seen you since Christmas. What brings you by?"

"We found a coal mine east of the Yourman Ranch. Do you know whose mine it was?"

"It was the Campbells who were digging it. They sunk several shafts in that area. They didn't find enough coal to call it a mine. They were a scheming lot. Arlie was the only one worth a hoot. Arlie was Jeremy Sean's grandfather. Oh boy, he loved to dance."

"We have a counterfeiter in the area. There was a printing press hidden in the mine shaft we found. A man saw us leaving the mine, and by the time the Sheriff got there, the press was gone. I believe he was at the Green Frog today and attempted to pass a counterfeit twenty. He was a tall thin man with thick black curly hair and blue eyes, about 50 years old."

"Stacie, that sounds like Jake Campbell. He grew up in Texas. Jake was always in trouble. He would come up here and stay when someone was after him in Texas. Earnest, my husband, found him snooping around here several times and would run him off."

Nellie pored more water for Will and Stacie and went over to the sink and hand pumped the pitcher full of water and placed it in the refrigerator. "You be careful if you see Jake. He has a mean streak."

Will and Stacie helped Nellie change a light bulb in the kitchen before they left.

Buckle and Pank were at the Community Building parking lot flying the Aeronca Champ that Pank had built over the winter. The Champ even had a camera that would take one picture, then the camera had to be wound to the next frame. Pank was into electronics. He could build anything. Pank was always reading Popular Science. Pank would order parts from Burstein-Applebee and Allied Radio, and voilà he had a radio controlled airplane, a radio or a walkie talkie.

Will and Stacie stopped and watched the Aeronca Champ fly. It was all line of sight. Pank let Buckle work the control and bring it in for a landing. The Champ had a 5 foot wing span. It could almost float forever. Buckle brought it in and cut the power. Pank walked as it floated down, catching it just above his head. Pank said, "You learn fast Buckle."

Buckle smiled and said nothing. Stacie caught Pank and Buckle up on all the news about Jake Campbell aka John Brown aka George Johnson. And Will told of the Raindrop mystery.

Pank commented, "I can buy a photo cell or an infrared sensor to make a camera take a picture of the person breaking into Miss Raindrop's house. Two weeks or less and I'll have it—not a problem. I'll even connect an electric bell that will ring when the light beam is disrupted. It will sound like a school bell."

Buckle said, "Let's go look for the mines tomorrow."

"Let's go to my house and get a drink. I'm thirsty," said Stacie.

Buckle said, "What about the mines?"

******

Jake Campbell was stopped outside of Hartshorne, OK at 3:21 p.m. and taken to the Latimer County Court House for questioning.

Jack Pratt, Treasury man, asked, "Where did you get the counterfeit twenty?"

Jake Campbell looked up toward the ceiling without moving his head. "I told you. I sold a gun to a man in Red Oak."

"Where's the twenty now?" Pratt questioned.

"I saw his car in Hartshorne and found him on the street. I got a good twenty from him. He has it now.

"Who has it?"

"The man I sold the gun to."

"What his name?"

"I didn't ask him."

Jack Pratt and Deputy Hawthorne walked out of the interrogation room.

"Marc, we are going to have to let him sit for awhile."

Marc said, "You saw how he was shifting his eyes and looking up at the ceiling. He is making it up as he goes."

******

Mrs. Robinson said, "Your Aunt Nancy told me how you identified a man from the description of the counterfeiter. I am proud of you Stacie."

"Thanks, Mom. Have you heard anything about Sydney's condition?"

"She is still unconscious—that poor girl."

Buckle questioned, "What are we going to do tomorrow?"

Pank said, "Look for the other lost mines."

Sadie Sawyer drives up to the Robinson house and approaches the group with a big smile. "Syd is out of the coma. She will be able to come home tomorrow. I want to thank you for finding her and knowing what to do. You saved her life."

Will said, "We did what we learned in 4H. We're just two kids."

"Well, Thank you both and I am sure Syd will thank you too."

Stacie asked, "What happened to her?"

"Sydney doesn't remember much; she was walking alone in the colony. You know it is just across the creek. She always walks with her billfold. She said a car pulled up alongside of her and a woman ask, if she knew where Steve Hill lives. That is the last thing she remembers. The doctor said she may never remember what happened, and she could remember it tomorrow."

Mrs. Robinson asked, "Who's Steve Hill?" No one knew.

Stacie said, "There are more questions now than before."

******

Pank said, "If the trail was wider we could take the Champ and take a picture of the area."

Buckle said, "It's a long walk, 3 hours in and 3 hours back. As it is, it may take all day. We had better take a lunch."

Will said' "I'll take my pack for exploring."

The next morning Pank was finished washing the breakfast dishes. It was his turn. Stacie and Buckle were on the road. As Pank hurried outdoors, Will was right behind him. The mine was barricaded with a sign DO NOT ENTER.

Pank said, "Let's divide this search area into four quadrants with the mine as the center starting point. Will, you and Stacie search the northeast quadrant and Buckle and I will go northwest quadrant."

After searching for about hour, both teams met up at the mines. Pank asked, "Did you find anything? We didn't." Stacie shook her head no. "Let's search to the south."

Pank and Buckle were walking side-by-side through an open area of the southwest quadrant. Without any warning, they stepped out into an abyss and fell down a dark shaft. Pank lifted Buckle to a standing position. The water had broken their fall. Pank was embarrassed that he screamed just as Buckle had. Pank said, "We found the mine shaft or this may be an old well."

The water was dark and stagnant. Buckle, who was not one to complain said, "What is that putrid odor?"

"It's dead animals and and rotting vegetation. Not to worry Will and Stacie will find us. We might be able to climb out. Are you okay? Nothings broken?"

"I'm fine in all this yuck; I hope we don't get sick," Buckle commented.

"Climb up on my shoulders. I think I can lift you up high enough that you can get out."

Buckle grabbed hold of Pank's hands and stepped on his knee. The area was tight and confining, but she stepped and turned to get both of her feet on his shoulders. Using the walls to stabilize her, Buckle stood up and stepped into Pank's hands. Pank lifted Buckle over his head. Her fingers were inches from the top. Buckle clawed the earth to reach freedom. Pank was showered with dirt as Buckle continued to attempt to climb out. Finally Buckle shouted, "Help! Help!" Buckle said, "Pank, let me down—it's no uses; We will have to wait until we are found. They took turns shouting for help every few minutes.

Will and Stacie returned and waited ten minutes, without a sign of Pank and Buckle. Stacie said, "I'll leave a note for them to stay put if they return. They may need help."

Ten minutes into the search, Stacie said, "I hear something. Listen." There were muffled cries for help. Will and Stacie walked toward the sound and there in the grass was a hole. Stacie peered down into the dim lighted hole. She could see Buckle, being the shorter was waist deep in water.

"Will throw us a rope," Pank said.

Will tied a bowline knot around a 4 inch oak tree and dropped the other end down the shaft. Buckle climbed up first and then came Pank.

Buckle said, "It's disgusting. We were looking for mine tailings and the next thing I know we were up to our necks in water. There were rotten animals down there with us."

"We can clean up at the pool. I hope we can get rid of the smell," Pank said.

Stacie said, "I have a bottle of rubbing alcohol in my pack. It will help, maybe after you wash at the pool, then we had better get back."

Will said, "There may be one more mine shaft here."

Buckle said, "Not today. I'm going to Mrs. Carter's and swim in the creek to get this yuck off of me. Grandfather will never let me leave the house if he see me like this."

By the time they finished swimming Pank and Buckle were feeling better. The smell was gone. Buckle and Pank were pleased with their adventure. "Pank and I were walking and down we fell in all that dark yucky water. It must have been twenty feet. We're lucky to be alive. It's something I'll never forget. Call me

Isabella from now on, that was a life changing experience. I feel older and more mature, now that I faced the Grim Reaper." Everyone laughed.

Stacie was thinking of how Jeremy Sean Campbell had showed up at the pavilion the morning that Sydney Sawyer was found. "Do you think Jeremy knows something about the counterfeit money? He seldom comes to the colony."

"He's a Campbell and Jake is his uncle. Go figure," Will said.

Pank said, "We could ride over to his house and see." It was a twenty minute bike ride over. The Damon Schoolhouse was vacant, but Pank commented on the path that went to the door. The tall Johnson grass was trampled down. It was being frequently traveled.

It was four o'clock and no one was home. As the four amateur detectives were leaving, they met Jeremy at the road in an old red Dodge pickup truck. "Hi, Jeremy. Is this a new pickup?" Will asked.

"No. It's Dad's. You know it has been in the barn. A friend helped me get it running," said Jeremy.

"Oh yeah. I forgot, Jeremy."

Stacie said, "Since you were interested in Sydney Sawyer, I thought you would want to know she is home now."

"I'm not interested in Sydney. What made you think that?"

"You showed up right after she was discovered. I thought you were concerned," Stacie said.

"No, I was out riding."

"You weren't concerned?"

"Well, yes, I'm concerned. Of course I'm concerned. Did she say what happened? Does she know who did it?"

Stacie said, "We don't know. Sydney doesn't remember, And no ones talking. Marc is as quiet as a clam."

"Oh."

Pank said, "Are you okay Jeremy? You don't look well."

"Do you know something you're not telling, Jeremy?" asked Buckle.

"No, I don't know anything about it."

"Jeremy, do you have an Uncle Jake?" Will asked.

"No. Yes, he's not here. I haven't seen him for awhile. Why? How do you know about him?"

Will said, "I hear things."

"You can't believe everything you hear. I have to make a phone call," Jeremy said.

Pank said, "We'll see you." As Jeremy drove toward the house.

The four were pedaling back to the colony, Isabella said, "That shook him up."

Stacie said, "What does it mean?"

"I believe he know's what happened to Sydney, and he was checking out the pavilion for something or someone. Jake Campbell is in the area. Who would the woman be that spoke with Sydney Sawyer?" Will said.

Pank commented, "The red truck Jeremy is driving could be the one that was at the mine. What do you think, Stacie?"

"I didn't see the truck it was parked behind a bunch of oak trees," Stacie reply.

******

Jack Pratt said, "Jake has a record. He has been arrested for robbery, assault, extortion—no convictions. He's smart. We don't have enough to make an arrest. Sheriff, we have to release him, unless you have something to charge him for."

Sheriff Latimer chuckling said, "Spitting on the sidewalk is a misdemeanor." They all laughed at the joke. "Marc, tell the Undersheriff to release the prisoner. Marc, let my deputies know not to follow Campbell, but report his whereabout when seen."

"Yes, sir." replied Marc.

"We'll need to catch him with counterfeit bills or the plates," Jack Pratt said.

******

"Sydney, are you going to tell me what happened?" Sadie said.

"Well Sadie, I met a man in town, David, last week. He looks like Elvis Presley. He's twenty-five and seemed really nice. We walked down to the post office. I mailed the letters and walked back. David went the other way."

"What does that have to do with you getting clobbered, Syd?"

"I'm not sure. There is a thought lingering in the back of my mind. Something, David, I don't know. I was walking around the colony, and a car pulled up to me. A woman ask directions."

"Where does David come into the picture? Was he in the car?"

"I don't know, Sadie. No, maybe, I don't know."

"Did you know you had a counterfeit twenty in your billfold?"

"I found it on the street just a little before David started talking to me. He ask what I had. I told him it was a twenty with writing on it."

"Do you know who hit you?"

"No, I was scared. I remember being chased. It was dark—not much of a moon. I ran down by the dam, hit a tree, dropped my wallet, and lost my watch. There was no time to look for them. I kept running and circled back to hide in the pavilion. Someone must have come from behind and hit me on the side of my head. I didn't see or hear anyone. It has something to do with David, maybe."

"Sydney, you need to write that down. We'll give it to Sheriff Latimer tomorrow."

"Sadie, there was a message written on the twenty dollar bill, and part of it was smudged so I couldn't read it."

"What did it say?"

"I want my plates or you're a dead man Joe M, or something like that—scary."

"Oh Boy, Sydney, we don't want to be messed up in counterfeiting."

Chapter 3

The order for the photo cell had been placed. Pank started building the circuit board for the automatic camera with an alarm. Pank was brilliant, but he kept it hidden very well. He was often referred to as the great silent one, which always brought a smile to his face.

"Will, we need to tap Jeremy Sean's phone line."

"Pank, it's against the law."

"It's Jeremy Sean's house. You hunt raccoon together. It will be like a practical joke. I have put your climbing gear in the truck and the portable repairman telephone that Dad found. All you have to do is climb the pole and hook the alligator clips to the lines, and I'll call Jeremy's number to be sure we have the right lines. You can come down and we wait for a call in or out. I checked out the line today while we were at Jeremy's."

"Okay. I'll get my climbing shoes."

"Mom, Can we take the truck over to Stacie's house? We may pick up Buckle and go to town and get a coke," Pank said.

"Be safe, and be back before ten," mother said.

In the pickup Pank said, "Buckle is at Stacie's. I've already talked to them, and they're expecting us."

"Don't forget she's Isabella, now. You like her, don't you?"

"I wish she was a year or two older. I can't date a 13 year old girl."

"Not to worry, Pank. She'll be fourteen someday."

Pank turned out the headlights, drove the last half mile in the moonlight, and parked the truck off the road in a pasture. The four sleuths walked the quarter mile to the pole that was sort of hidden by trees. "That's the pole I selected."

Will Ballad shinnied up the pole, ankles looped and safety line technique. The leads were 30 foot, which was plenty long for the group to hide in the trees.

Pank was dead on. He knew exactly which lines to connect the alligator clips. Pank rang Jeremy's number. Jeremy answered the phone. Pank disguised his voice and pulled a name out of the air; he said, "Is Joe there?" Jeremy said, "Wrong number," and hung up. Will shinnied down the pole.

Jeremy placed a call to the Sky View Motel, cabin #6. The call was transferred and Jake picked up the line. "Jake, Joe called."

"How do you know it was Joe Marciano?"

"I don't. They asked for Joe," Jeremy said. "I said, "Wrong number, and hung up."

"They may know where I am. The Treasury man had me picked up. Joe has eyes and ears everywhere. Do you still have the package?

"Yes."

"Don't go near it. It's too dangerous. Joe wants it and the Treasury men want it. I will have to lay low for awhile. I'll be in touch."

"Jake did you hurt Sydney Sawyer?" Jeremy asked.

Jake opened up, "It was a mistake. Sal Valentino is Joe's man. He's mean. Sal thought she was connected to me somehow. I got in over my head. You should take the canoe down Gaines Creek and fish for a couple of days."

"I'll do that Jake."

"Jeremy where is the package?"

"It is the ghost tree."

"Will Ballad knows where the ghost tree is, if I'm not around."

"Son of a gun," Will whispered.

"Get out of there," the line went dead.

"Sorry," Will said.

Pank yanked the leads from the field telephone leaving two wires hanging and said, "We've got to get, too."

Will held the barbed wire fence. Pank and the girls went through. Will tore his jeans hurrying between the wires. They jogged down the road to the pickup truck and were gone.

Stacie asked, "What's the ghost tree?"

Will answered, "Jeremy and I hunt coon in the winter. There is an old oak tree that the top is broken off. The top is hollow for about two feet. An old raccoon will hide there when the dogs get too close. It is a free base for the coon. We like the chase more than killing the raccoons. So we named it the ghost tree. It is up on the Henderson place at the base of Blue Mountain."

Stacie and Buckle said, "We want to go coon hunting," in unison.

Pank said, "We need to tell Marc. This is important."

"You can tell Marc. Wiretapping is illegal. We'll go to jail. Pank, let's go home first and dump the gear. We can walk the girls up the hill, since Buckle is spending the night with Stacie."

As the four were walking up the hill, the law came over the top lights flashing. It was Marc—he hit the brakes and slid past the foursome.

Will spoke in his most important voice, with fear in his heart that they were found out. "Hi Marc. Are you in a hurry?"

"Where have you been?"

"We're walking the girls home, Marc. Isabella is spending the night with Stacie."

Jack Pratt, the Treasury man, wants to talk to you."

"Just me."

"No I think I'll take you all in. Climb in, we'll go to your house and make some calls."

Marc explained everything to the parents and Mr. Martinez, Isabella's grandfather. The four rode with Marc, lights flashing.

At the Latimer County Courthouse, Jack Pratt spoke with Will, Pank, Stacie, Isabella and their guardians; he explained that Joe Marciano was a gangster on the East Coast. Marciano had been tapping Jeremy Sean Campbell's telephone. Jeremy's Uncle, Jake Campbell, had stolen counterfeiting plates and counterfeit twenty dollar bills from Joe Marciano.

Jack Pratt continued explaining, "Sydney Sawyer was chased and knock out as a message to the Campbells, because they thought she was involved with Jake Campbell. She had the counterfeit twenty that the note was written: I want my plates back. You have 2 days or you're a dead man Joe M. It was apparently a mistake."

"Joe called Jeremy Sean Campbell tonight and asked for himself to scare Jeremy into calling Jake Campbell." Will looked at Pank. Mr. Pratt continued to inform the group,

"Jeremy told Jake that Will Ballad knew where the ghost tree was and that Will could find the package if anything happened to him. Will, we feel that you and your friends are in danger until this is resolved."

"Will, can you show us the ghost tree," Mr. Pratt asked.

"Tonight? It's dark. Have you ever been in the woods at night?"

Jack Pratt didn't answer the question. He replied, "I want eyes on it as soon as possible."

Will took a chance and said, "Deputy Hawthorne is a good man in the wood. Can he go with me?"

"Sheriff Latimer has given the full cooperation of his department to help with the mission," Jack Pratt said.

Deputy Sheriff Marc Hawthorne and Deputy Sheriff Jerry Jones were ready to go. Will explained, "We can be dropped off at the top of Blue Mountain and walk the ridge to get to the huge rock slide. From there we will be able to see the ghost tree."

It was past 1:00 a.m. The moon was bright in the sky. Will pointed down the huge rock slide. It was one big rock, 600 feet across and 300 foot down and some places as steep as a 70° angle. The rock was spotted with a blueish green lichen. Will slid down and the Deputies followed. As the ground began to level two hundred feet below them, Will said, "See the light in the valley, that's the Henderson place—follow it straight back to the base of the mountain. See the large blackjack tree with the top broken? It is about 12 inches in diameter and 15 feet high. That's the ghost tree, gentlemen," Will said.

Marc removed his pack and passed water around. He dug in his pack for his binoculars. "I can't see if anything is still there," Marc said.

Will said, "The hole is deep and a raccoon can hide in it. If you intend to stake it out, you'll have to be hidden in the trees. You're visible up here."

The three continued down and found a place to hide. Marc said, "Jerry you stay here. I'll walk Will out and see that he gets home. You hold this position. You have water, food and a radio. No fires, no smoking. If anyone should come tonight monitor them, do not try to apprehended them alone. You're on radio silence so wait to be contacted. We'll do radio checks every hour on the hour. I'll be back as quick as I can. Jerry, tell me what I said."

You said, "I have food, water and a radio. No fires, no smoking. If anyone should come tonight, monitor them, do not try to apprehend them alone. And that I'm on radio silence. And to do radio check on the hour; I'm to wait to be contacted."

"Jerry, you will be notified if you are being approached. I'll be back in an hour."

Will led Marc out behind the Henderson's home. They came out on the road a mile north of the Damon

Schoolhouse. Will and Marc hid in the brushes until an unmarked pickup truck stopped in front of them. Marc said, "Thank you for the help. This will be over soon. I'll see you after this is over."

Will was feeling pretty important at the moment, but he quickly remembered Pank, Isabella and Stacie were a big part of the attention he received. Will was smart enough to realize he was part of a team. It was a great feeling to be a part of a team. A team was what they had formed. Will wanted to continue to be with his friends.

After Marc returned, he climb the tree to check the package. There were counterfeiting plates, a fair amount of counterfeit twenties, and a Smith and Wesson .38 revolver sealed in oilcloth and then in canvas. Marc took the cartridges out of the revolver.

Three days later Pank and Isabella took pictures with the Aeronca Champ. Pank had to rewind after each picture. They took three, the Damon Schoolhouse, Jeremy's house and the ghost tree. Pank missed the ghost tree, and had a picture of a whiskey still in the woods. "Isabella, we will have to think about who is working this still. We don't want to rile someone. There are barn burners in this part of Oklahoma. Marc has probably already found it."

Marc and Jerry were self sufficient on stakeout eating C-rations. Marc told Jerry, "I thought these days were behind me." Marc had explored the area and found a pool. They used iodine tablets to kill the viruses, fungus and bacteria.

There was a trail leading from the pond that led directly to a whiskey still. There were barrels of sour mash that would soon be ready to cook. When this stake out was over the Sheriff may or may not catch the cooker. The politics was strange in Southeastern Oklahoma. The people were poor. Some families survived off of whiskey sales. The people elected the sheriff. All the sheriff had to do was wait for the smoke, that would be when the owner of the still would be cooking. Marc wasn't sure what would happen. The still would be destroyed? Was the cooker tipped off or would he show up and be arrested? Politics and family ties ran deep throughout the county.

It had been almost a week since the stakeout started. The photo cell arrived, and Pank completed the circuit board. He mounted it in a small wood box. The camera was attached to a board. Once the circuit was triggered in the photo cell, the master would send a signal to the slave, the camera would take the picture and the alarm would ring.

Miss Judy Raindrop was excited to see the four visitors. Isabella was fascinated with Miss Raindrop's huge house. Pank set the camera up and instructed Miss Raindrop how to use it. "All you have to do is turn the toggle switch on when you leave the house," Pank said. He added, "If you forget and trip the camera, turn it off, and advance the film to the next frame. You can switch it on again when you're ready to leave; it is ready to go. The bell is plugged into the outlet so it will ring until it is shut off."

Miss Raindrop said, "Thank you so much. I want to find out who is stealing from me."

"When you have an intruder, call me; we're in the phonebook. I'll come to get the film and develop it that night."

"I will, and thank you again."

******

"Black Jack this is Rover, over."

"Rover, this is Black Jack, what do you have? over."

"Black Jack this is Rover. Three bogeys are coming your way. It's Salvatore Valentino and another man. Jeremy Campbell has his hands tied behind his back. Over."

"Rover, this is Black Jack, we are ready. We are going silent. I don't want them to hear the radio. Out."

Marc whispered, "Jerry, this should be simple. They will probably make Jeremy climb the tree. I'll move ten yards south so we will be separated and have them in a vector. Once Jeremy gets above them, I'll call them out. You'll know to shoot if they're uncooperative."

"This is the ghost tree," Jeremy said.

"Where's our plates?" Sal said.

"They're hidden in the hole at the top."

"Don't just stand there, climb the tree and get the plates."

"I can't."

Sal slaps Jeremy across the head. "What do you mean, you can't."

"My hands are tied."

"That's a good one." Sal said laughing, "His hands are tied Joey." Joey cut him loose. "Sal said, "Now, get up there. I been out here too long already."

Jeremy was half way up the tree. "The kid's a squirrel too bad we have shoot him," Joey said.

Marc takes a bead. "This is the Sheriff. Drop your guns."

Sal raises the semi automatic Colt .45 in Marc's direction. Marc fires two to the chest. Sal falls to the ground. Joey throws his revolver on the ground and raises his hands.

"Jerry, call it in," Marc said. "Jeremy, get down."

"Don't you want me to bring the package down?"

Marc said, "No. That's our job. I don't know what's up there. You may have a gun. Get down here."

Jeremy jumps down. Mark and Jerry secure the two prisoner. Sal is alive. Marc's two bullets hit Sal high in the shoulder. Marc administered first aid.

Sal said, "You shot me."

Marc said, "You didn't drop your gun. You're alive and have a long life ahead of you. The arm won't be as good as it was, but I think you will have some use still."

Sheriff Latimer, Jack Pratt and six other men showed up. Jack sent a Treasury man up the tree. Marc handed the Sheriff his semi auto Colt .45. The stakeout was over.

Sal had to be carried out on a stretcher. Jeremy Sean Campbell wasn't charged with any crime. He was released. Jake Campbell had made a clean get-away. Jeremy's mother said that Jake was slick; he always was one step ahead of the law.

Pank showed Marc the pictures he took with the model Champ, and Marc showed the Sheriff. Marc and the Sheriff were amazed that a high school student could build a radio controlled airplane, yet fly it and take pictures. Sheriff Latimer said, "Someday, radio controlled airplanes would be a big part of law enforcement."

No one ever showed up to cook the sour mash. The whiskey still was destroyed. Pank's picture was run with the story in the Wilburton newspaper. Pank was very apprehensive, wondering if someone would seek revenge.

After the article in the newspaper, Bob Trout actually paid Pank to help him build a model radio controlled airplane and to instruct him in flying it. Pank told Mr. Trout, "The technology is there for a camera to take more than one picture without landing; I don't have the funds to create it."

Bob Trout said, "If it's money you need, I can help you there." A partnership was being formed.

Two days after the shoot out at the ghost tree, Judy called Pank to let him know someone had broken into her home. True to his word, Pank drove in picked up the film, reloaded the camera, just in case of a malfunction.

The photo after Pank blew it up to an 8 X 10 showed Dizzy Dryer half way out of a secret trap door in the floor, that was built so well Judy did not know it was there. The trap door led to a passage way that went under the house to Judy Raindrop's grandfather's,

Clay Mobley, workshop. He hated tracking mud and dirt in his wife's kitchen.

The four went back to town, and Pank showed the picture to Miss Raindrop. She immediately walked the three blocks to Dizzy's house and got her possessions back. Dizzy was scared away by the bell, and knew he was in trouble. Dizzy was an old man. Miss Raindrop understood Dizzy needed help. She told him to come by in the morning she had a job for him.

Miss Raindrop said, "Please help me seal off this passageway." Pank lead the way down into to the passage. There was a hasp on the swinging wall. Pank slid a half inch bolt in the hasp to secure the wall.

Judy Raindrop wanted to pay Pank for this help. Pank said what dad always said when he helped someone, and they wanted to pay him. "Just help the next person who needs help and it will be pay enough for me."

As Will had done so many times before, he walked up to Stacie's. The moon was full. Stacie was still awake reading. They talked about the summer and their friendship. Will put his hand on the screen and Stacie put her hand against his. They could feel the warmth of their friendship between the cold steel screen as the two hands touch.

"Good night, Stacie."

"Good night, Will Ballad."

Before Will went home, he wrote a note on the 3 X 5 card he carried in his pocket. He carefully hid the note in the cavity of their secret rock across the road from Stacie's house. It said: Splendid summer, Sunshine!

Will thought, time flies far too fast when you're having fun.

About the Author

Oak Blackheart graduated from the University of Oklahoma. He is a retired teacher who wrote stories for his fourth grade students. Oak Blackheart wrote "Pedaling Through the Past," articles about bicyclists rediscovering ghost towns in Pottawatomie County, OK for the *Shawnee News Star.*

Oak is a mountain bike rider and lives in Oklahoma and New Mexico. Blackheart grew up in Southeastern Oklahoma. He served in the U.S. Coast Guard and retired from the U.S. Army. He continues to share stories with his granddaughter.

wiltonp.blogspot.com

Facebook: Oak Blackheart

www.ingramcontent.com/pod-product-compliance
Lightning Source LLC
Chambersburg PA
CBHW020643130626
46552CB00003B/1372